Disney

Bibbidi Bobbidi Academy

Mai and the Tricky Transformation

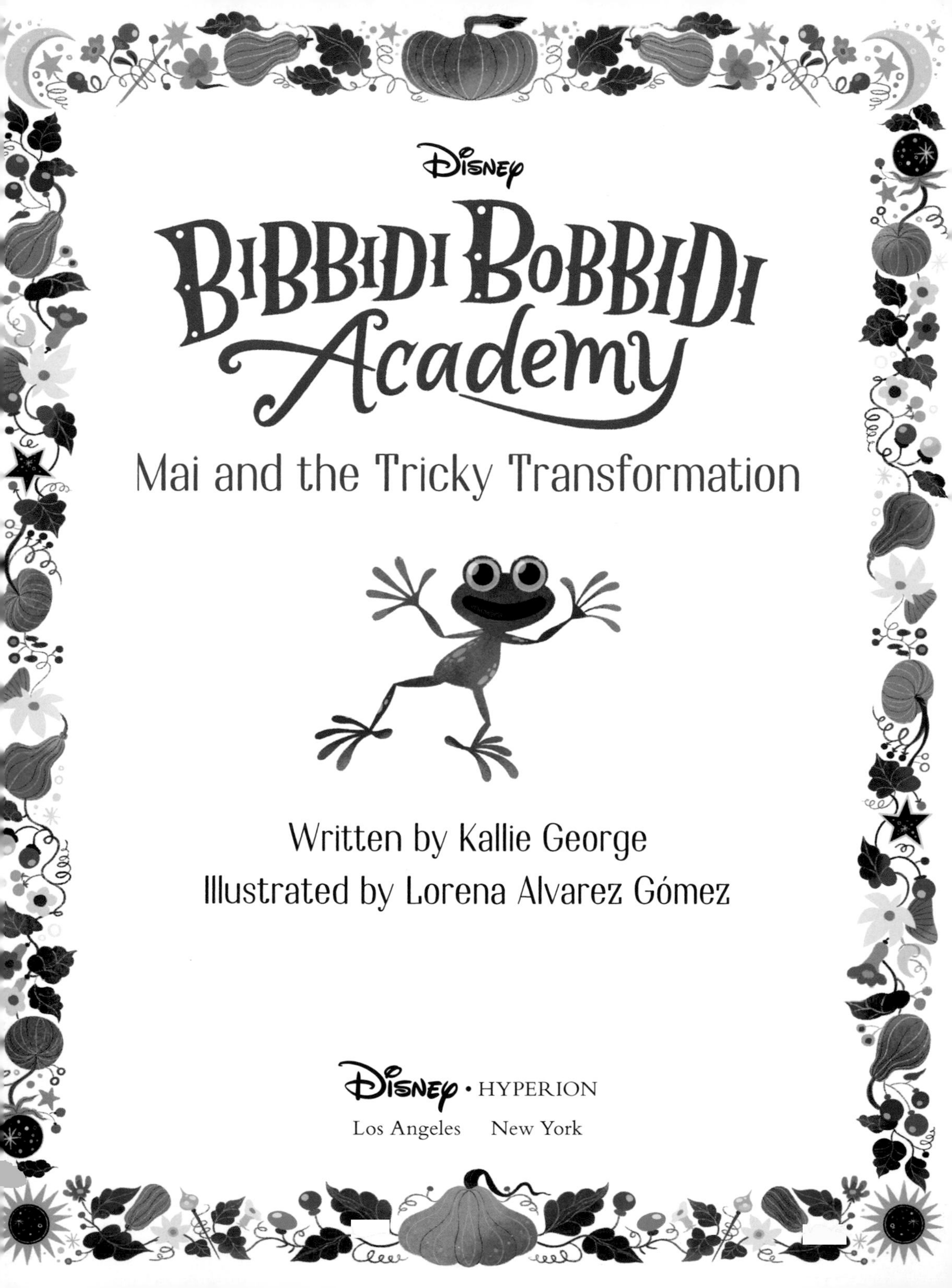

Disney

Bibbidi Bobbidi Academy

Mai and the Tricky Transformation

Written by Kallie George
Illustrated by Lorena Alvarez Gómez

Disney • HYPERION
Los Angeles New York

First Edition, October 2022
1 3 5 7 9 10 8 6 4 2
FAC-004510-22238
Printed in the United States of America

Library of Congress Control Number: 2021950237
ISBN 978-1-368-05788-2

Visit www.DisneyBooks.com

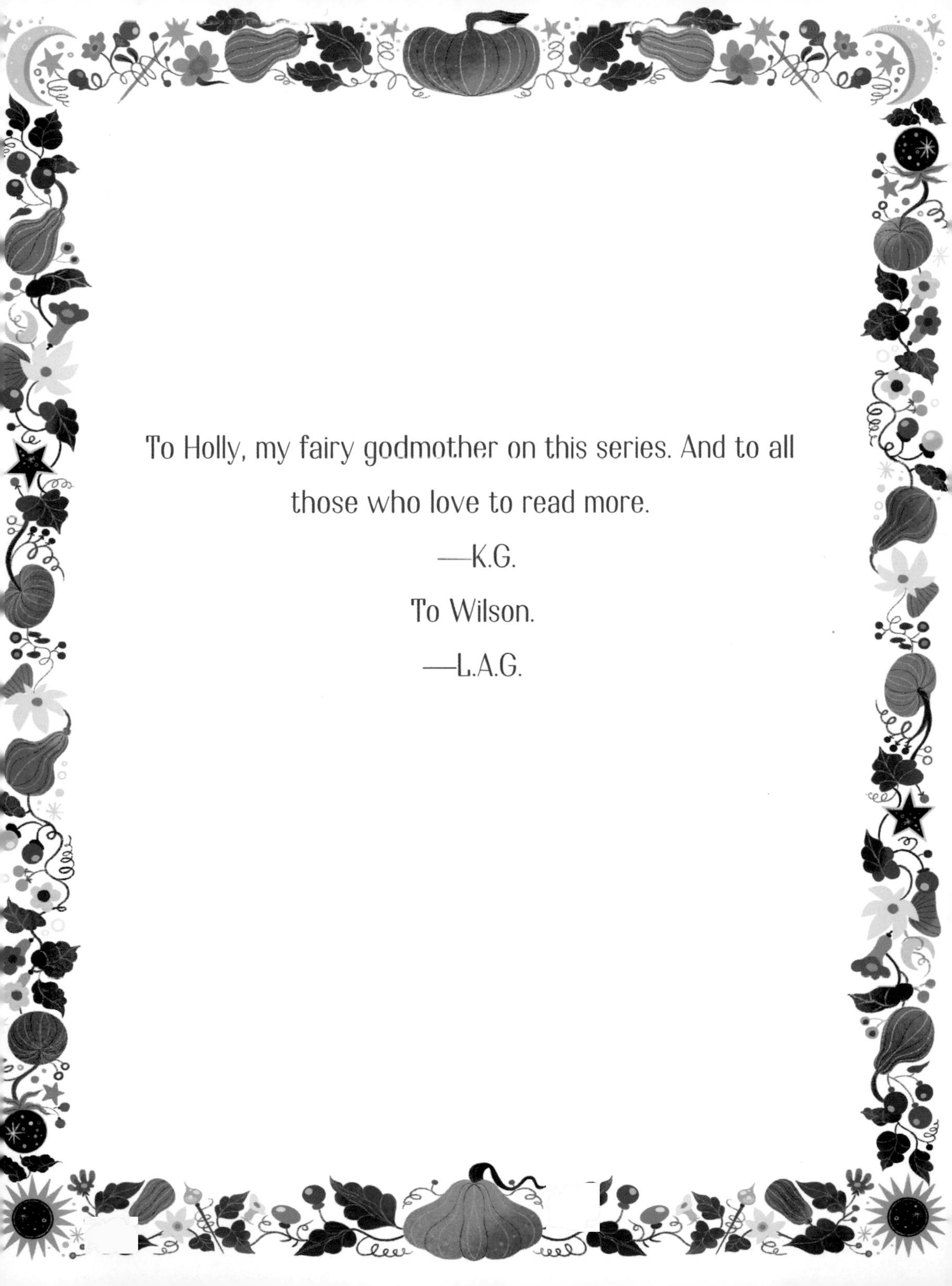

To Holly, my fairy godmother on this series. And to all those who love to read more.

—K.G.

To Wilson.

—L.A.G.

Bibbidi Bobbidi Academy

CHAPTER 1
Mai Magicwhisp

Mai Magicwhisp's motto was *more.*

More Bibbidi.

More Bobbidi.

More Boo!

Bibbidi Bobbidi Boo was what fairy godmothers said to make a spell come true.

Bibbidi Bobbidi was also the name of Mai's school.

Right now she was a fairy-godmother-in-training.

Training was tricky.

Mai's first assignment hadn't gone so well.

She was supposed to grant a child's wish. But the crown she spelled wasn't what he wanted. Maybe if she had done more. More of what, she wasn't sure.

Tonight was her second chance.

Tonight was the Midterm Ball. She and the other students would spend the day making their best transformations for visiting princesses and princes. Just like how the Fairy Godmother, their headmistress, had changed Cinderella's rags into a beautiful gown.

Unlike the Fairy Godmother, however, the students were making their transformations ahead of time, so there would be no trouble.

Mai wasn't sure what she would be assigned to make yet.

But she WAS sure she would do more than enough to complete it perfectly.

First, though, she had to get ready.

Her uniform was nice, but . . . it needed something more.

Mai waved her wand and said the magic words.

"Bibbidi Bobbidi Boo!"

Once, twice, three times.

More spots.

Poof!

More stripes.

Poof!

More sparkles.

"How do I look?" she asked Rory. Rory Spellington was Mai's roommate and her best friend. Rory wasn't very good at magical spelling; still, she had completed their first assignment.

"Bright?" Rory blinked.

"Brilliant," said Mai. In fact, she was SO sparkly, she could barely see. Mai spelled a pair of sunglasses.

Poof!

Perfect!

Now, she was more than ready.

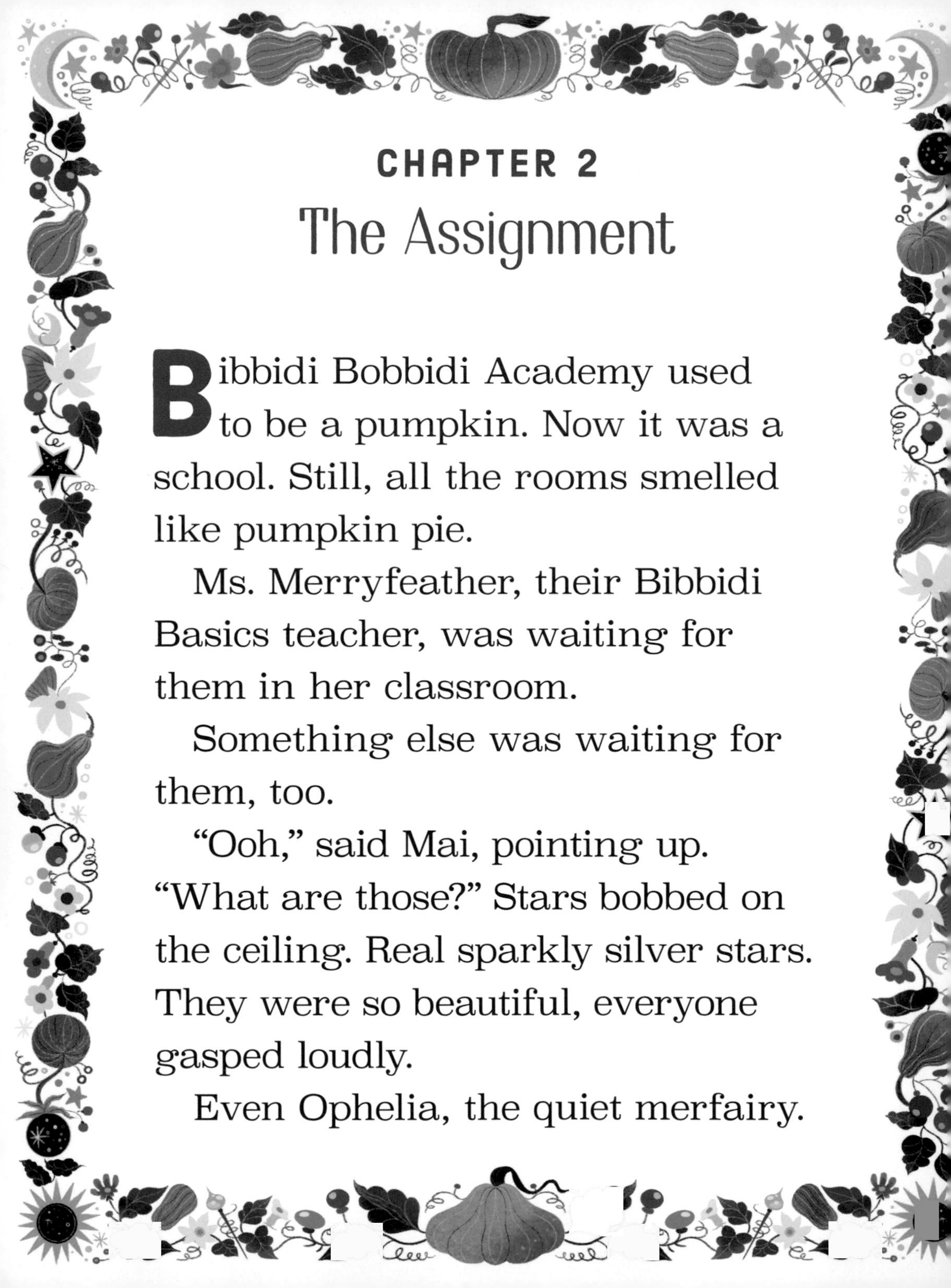

CHAPTER 2

The Assignment

Bibbidi Bobbidi Academy used to be a pumpkin. Now it was a school. Still, all the rooms smelled like pumpkin pie.

Ms. Merryfeather, their Bibbidi Basics teacher, was waiting for them in her classroom.

Something else was waiting for them, too.

"Ooh," said Mai, pointing up. "What are those?" Stars bobbed on the ceiling. Real sparkly silver stars. They were so beautiful, everyone gasped loudly.

Even Ophelia, the quiet merfairy.

"Should those be inside?" worried Cyrus, one of the fairy-godfathers-in-training.

Tatia answered first. "Of course. I know what they are."

Tatia Shine was always first, except during their last magical assignment. Like Mai, she hadn't granted a wish.

"Those stars add twinkles to your wand."

Right now, the students' wands only went *poof*. They didn't twinkle.

"Twinkles are a sign of a *real* fairy godmother," Tatia went on. "My sister got lots of stars when she was at the Academy."

Ms. Merryfeather stepped in. "Very good, Tatia," she said. "But first you must complete your assignment to earn a star."

Now Mai was even more determined to do her best. If she had a star everyone would see she was a good fairy-godmother-in-training. A star was the perfect, prettiest proof.

"Please pick a partner," continued their teacher.

Mai jumped up to find Rory.

She found Tatia instead.

Tatia had stood up first, as usual.

"Very good. You two can go together," said Ms. Merryfeather.

Oh no!

Mai wanted to be partners with Rory!

Still, Mai tried to stay bright.

"We can make the dresses. And the shoes. And even more . . ." she said.

"You and Tatia will make *one* thing," said Ms. Merryfeather. "You will be in charge of the coach."

"The coach?" asked Tatia.

"Transportation, for the princesses- and princes-in-training," Ms. Merryfeather explained. "It's tradition for them to ride home in a carriage. You will need to transform a suitable vegetable and bring it back by four o'clock. That's when the Fairy Godmother and I will be reviewing all the assignments, before you present them to our guests. Now, for the other teams . . ."

But Mai had stopped paying attention.

Her head was filled with stars, and her wings were flapping as fast as her thoughts.

“Come on,” she said to Tatia.

But Tatia was already out the door.

CHAPTER 3

The Practice Patch

Mai followed Tatia to the Practice Patch.

The Practice Patch was filled with fruits and vegetables. Pumpkins. And carrots. And even purple cabbages.

Purple cabbages were the most glamorous, decided Mai.

She gathered as many as she could.

Tatia picked a single pea.

"Let's use this," said Tatia.

“No, these,” argued Mai, pointing to her pile.

“Fine,” huffed Tatia. “But *I* will go first.”

Tatia waved her wand and said the magic words. The pile of cabbages turned into a coach.

A completely classic coach.

The coach was nice, but . . . it needed something more.

Mai waved her wand and said, "Bibbidi Bobbidi Boo!"

Once, twice, three times.

More bells.

Poof!

More bows.

Poof!

More balloons.

POOF!

Actually, there were no balloons. But Mai added some.

POOF!

"Okay. It looks good. Let's go," said Tatia. "I want to finish first."

"No. It's still too ordinary. We have lots of time. We need to do something more. That's my motto," said Mai. She waved her wand.

The cabbages changed.
Again, again, and again!
Even the pea got involved!

"Enough," said Tatia. "I want to complete the assignment this time. Don't you?"

Mai did. Of course she did. "But just one more spell. Actually, all of my spells. That will make the MOST magical transformation ever!"

"Stop!" cried Tatia. She flitted in front of Mai.

Too late . . .

Mai waved her wand and thought of all her most sparkly spells and said the magic words.

Once, twice . . . TEN times!

POOF! POOF!! POOF!!!

When the cloud of magic cleared, the coach was gone.

And so was Tatia.

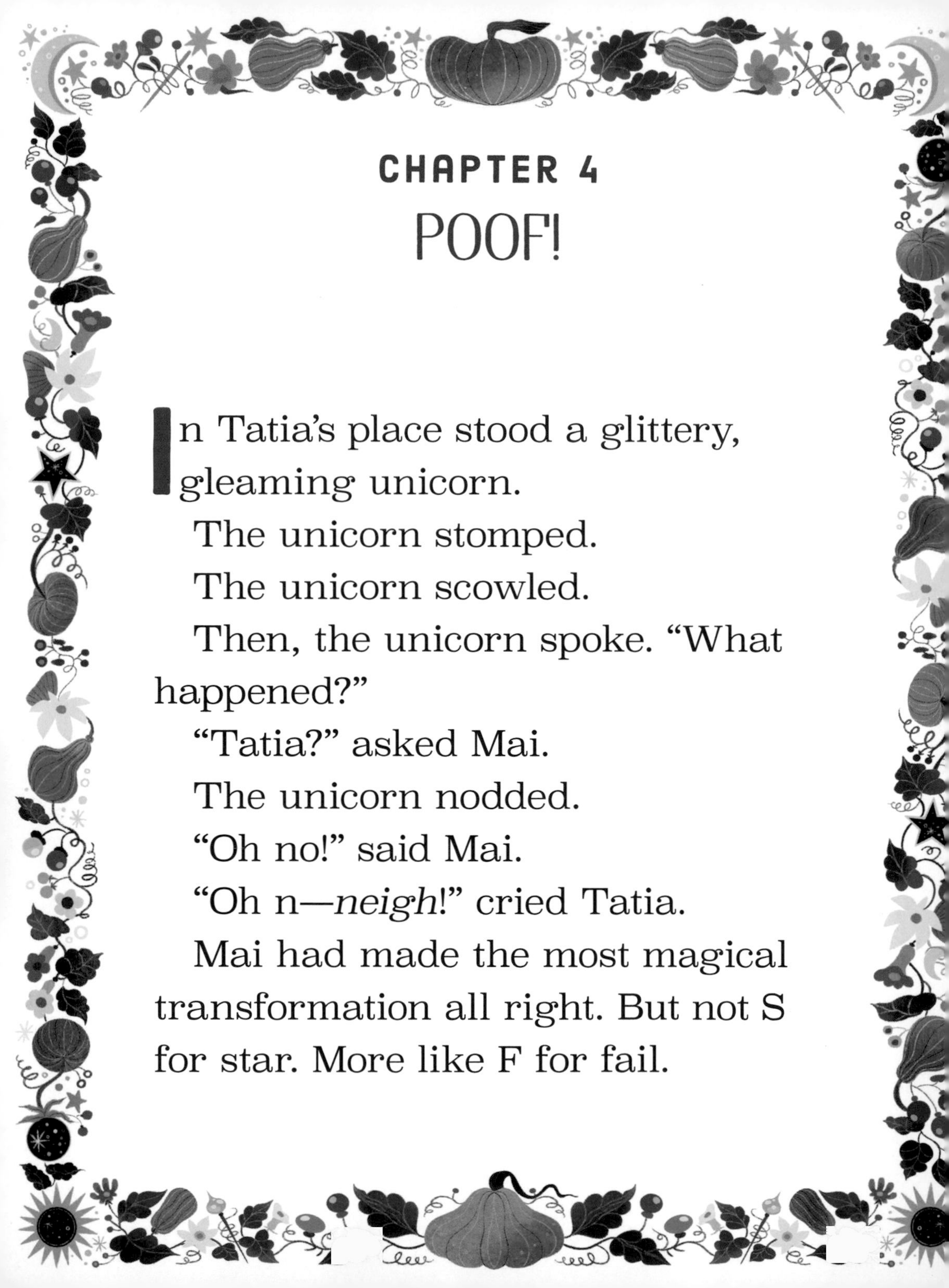

CHAPTER 4

POOF!

In Tatia's place stood a glittery, gleaming unicorn.

The unicorn stomped.

The unicorn scowled.

Then, the unicorn spoke. "What happened?"

"Tatia?" asked Mai.

The unicorn nodded.

"Oh no!" said Mai.

"Oh n—*neigh*!" cried Tatia.

Mai had made the most magical transformation all right. But not S for star. More like F for fail.

"Change me back, right now!" Tatia demanded.

Mai didn't know how. She never undid her work. She only did more.

But she could try. She waved her wand.

Only fizzles came from it.

And now, Mai thought with a gulp, twinkles never would.

"We just need some help," said Mai. "Come with me."

"Are you kidding? N—*neigh* one can see me like this. *You* find Ms. Merryfeather," ordered Tatia. "Only *don't* tell her it's for me. Just find out how to undo this."

"Don't worry," said Mai. "I'll fix it!"

And off she flew.

CHAPTER 5

The Story Shed

Inside the school, all Mai found were stars and students.

"Have you seen Ms. Merryfeather?" asked Mai.

Rory and Cyrus were hard at work. They shook their heads.

Ophelia, who loved to help, said, "All the teachers are in the Story Shed setting up. You might find her there. Good luck."

"Thank you," said Mai. She needed it!

The Story Shed was shaped like a big book, resting on its pages. When you went inside, it often told a different story. Today, it looked like a ballroom.

The teachers were busy decorating. Even Ms. Ebony, their history teacher and a retired witch, was arranging thorns in vases. But where was Ms. Merryfeather?

Mai asked Ms. Ebony.

"She's off to fetch the princes and princesses," explained their teacher. "How's your assignment going?"

"Well." Mai gulped. "It's . . . tricky."

Ms. Ebony cackled. "When I was a witch, I just loved tricky transformations. What I didn't like was everything that undid them."

"Really?" said Mai. "Like what?"

Ms. Ebony scratched the wart on the end of her nose. "Hmm. Like fairy-tale kisses," she said. "Or the stroke of midnight.

There was also that princess who broke a curse by cutting her hair.

And another did by crying tears." She scowled at the thought.

Mai, on the other hand, smiled.

"Thank you, Ms. Ebony. You helped me a lot!"

Ms. Ebony looked confused, but Mai just waved and turned around.

Now she had enough ideas to help Tatia.

More than enough.

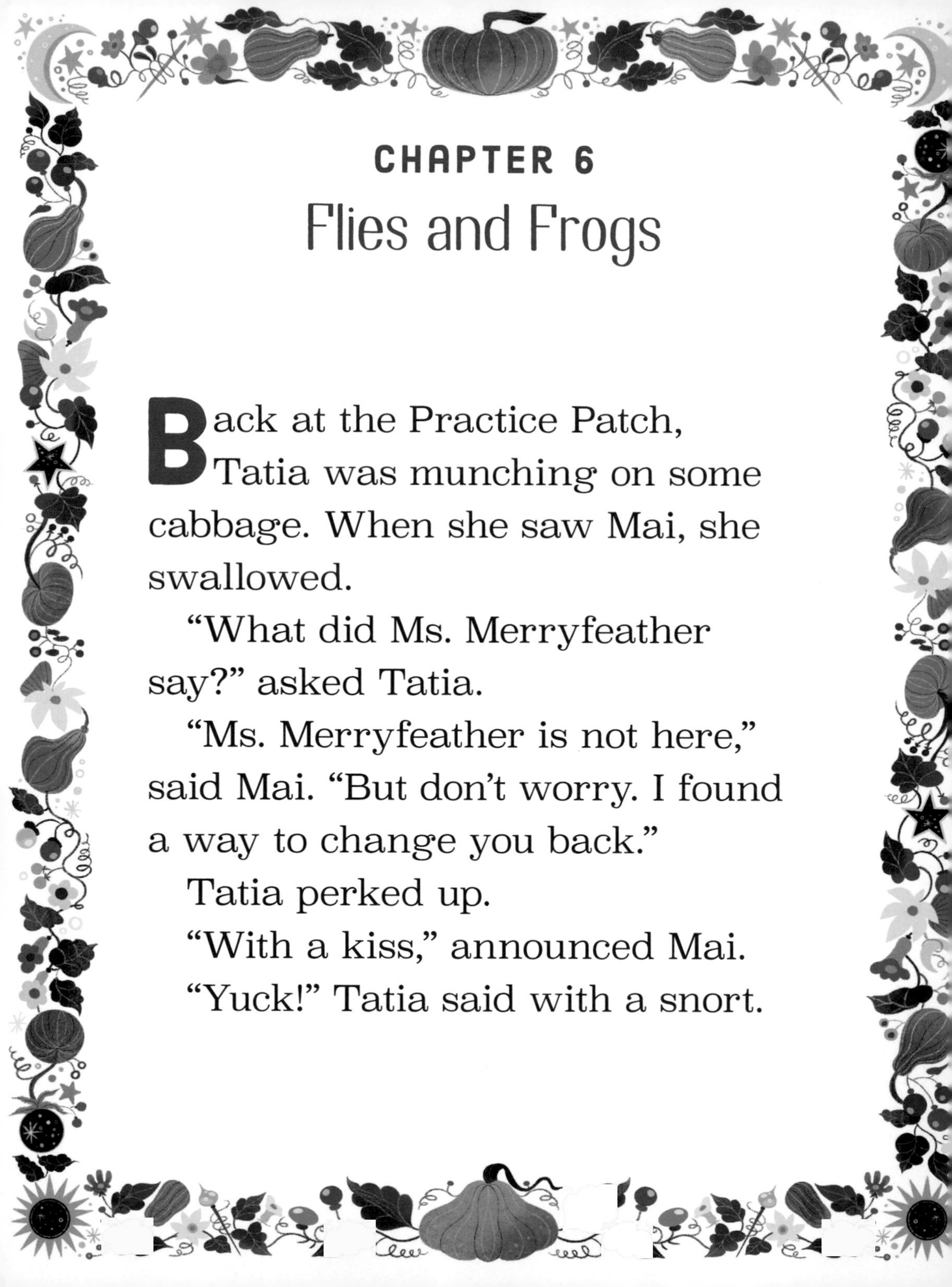

CHAPTER 6
Flies and Frogs

Back at the Practice Patch, Tatia was munching on some cabbage. When she saw Mai, she swallowed.

"What did Ms. Merryfeather say?" asked Tatia.

"Ms. Merryfeather is not here," said Mai. "But don't worry. I found a way to change you back."

Tatia perked up.

"With a kiss," announced Mai.

"Yuck!" Tatia said with a snort.

Mai ignored her.

She waved her wand and said the magic words.

A whistle appeared. Mai blew it. She heard a splash from the Playground Pond.

Soon, a frog hopped toward them.

"In fairy tales, kissing a frog always changes a spell," she explained.

Mai paused.

One frog was good. But more might be better.

Mai blew the frog whistle again. And again.

"Double yuck!" said Tatia. "I would *neigh*—never kiss a frog."

Too late . . . More were coming.
More green ones. *Hop!*
More warty ones. *Hop!*
More hoppy ones! *HOP!*

"Help!" cried Tatia. "Do something."

Mai thought quickly.

She waved her wand and . . . "Bibbidi Bobbidi Boo!"

Bzzz! A fly appeared. Then more and more.

Soon there was a big cloud of them.

The frogs hopped toward the flies.

The fairies flew in the opposite direction.

Well, one fairy flew.

The other trotted, her tail swishing behind her.

CHAPTER 7
Tisk-Tock

"Ding-dong! One o'clock," the School Clock chimed ahead of them.

"We don't have much time left," worried Tatia.

Time! That was it! Mai stopped at the Clock.

The Clock was big. And old. And a bit of a grump.

Sometimes it even skipped recess!

Still, Mai flew up to it.

“I guess a kiss IS an old-fashioned way to solve the problem,” puffed Mai. “But *this* is perfect.”

Tatia looked up. “It’s just the School Clock.”

“Exactly,” said Mai. “Some transformations change back at the stroke of midnight. Like with Cinderella’s dress and coach.”

“We can’t wait till midnight,” said Tatia.

“I know,” agreed Mai, “but we can MAKE it midnight. Just for a moment. We can trick the spell by turning the Clock forward. Then turn the Clock back.”

Mai turned the Clock’s hands once, twice, three times.

The Clock cried, “Ouch! Ouch! Ouch!”

"Sorry," apologized Mai. "But I *really* need to do this."

She tried to move its hands some more. The Clock wouldn't budge.

"TISK-TOCK, TISK-TOCK!" it chimed more loudly.

"What is going on?" called a familiar voice.

It was the Fairy Godmother!

Quickly, Mai and Tatia hid.

"Oh, dear me, you are a grump," they heard the Fairy Godmother say. "I think that's the last time I make a clock from a stump. Uncross those hands. Now, what time was it?"

The Fairy Godmother was a bit forgetful.

They heard the Clock complain as the Fairy Godmother adjusted the time. Then, at last, it was quiet.

Mai and Tatia peeked out.

The Fairy Godmother was gone.

"Ding-dong! Two o'clock," the Clock chimed again, with a smirk.

Oh no! The Fairy Godmother had turned it one hour ahead.

Now they had even *less* time to make things right.

CHAPTER 8

No More!

"We will NEVER be first to get a star now," cried Tatia. "We probably won't even finish."

But Mai wasn't ready to give up.

"I have two more ideas," she said.

Still, two wasn't a lot.

Her hand trembled as she waved her wand.

This time she made a pair of scissors.

They were a bit dull, but they were eager to snip.

"Sometimes a haircut reverses magic," explained Mai. "Like with Rapunzel."

"I guess," said Tatia, uncertain. "But just a little."

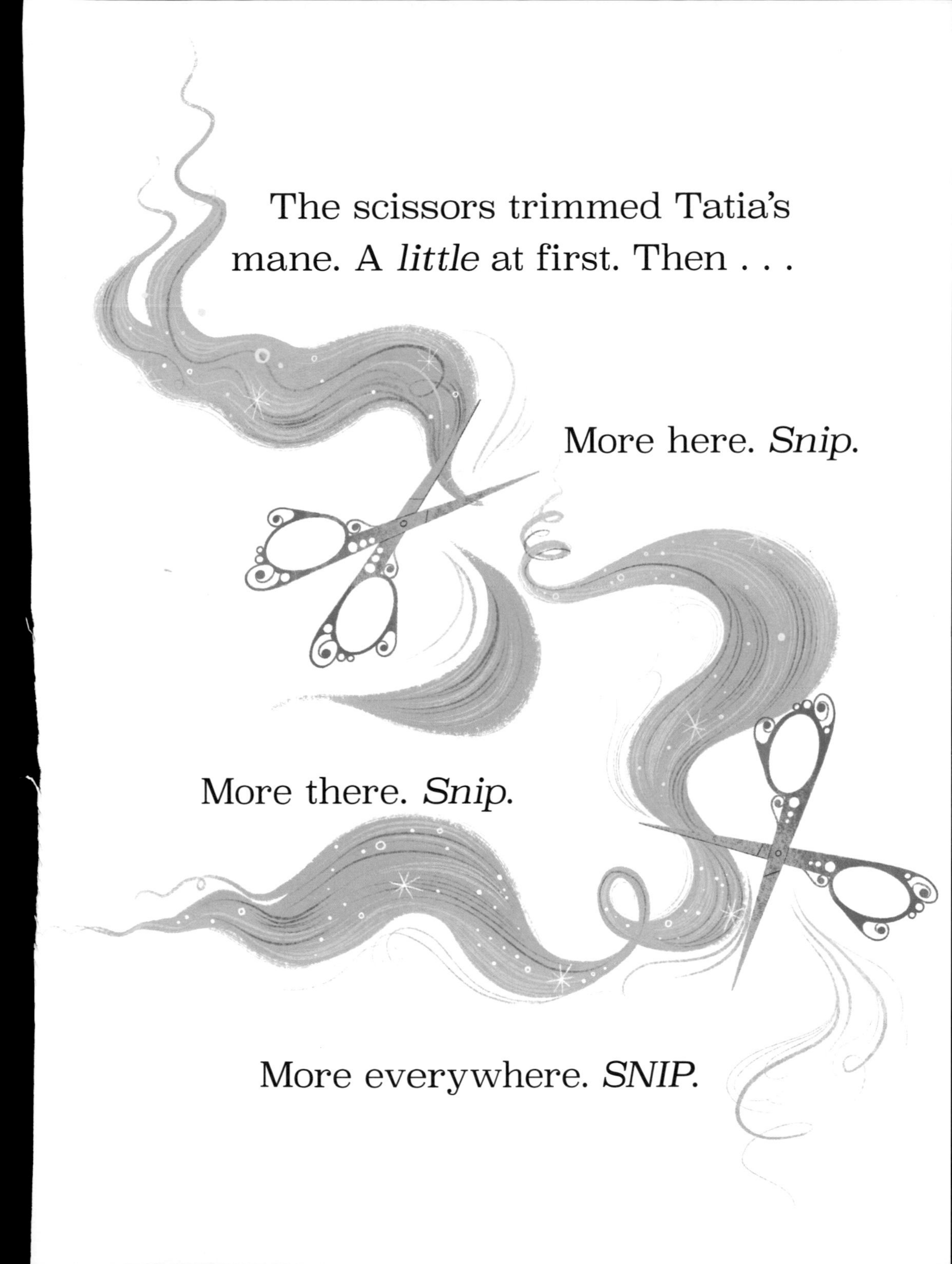

The scissors trimmed Tatia's mane. A *little* at first. Then . . .

More here. *Snip.*

More there. *Snip.*

More everywhere. *SNIP.*

"STOP!" whinnied Tatia. "Now I'm a unicorn AND I have no hair."

Mai felt bad. And a bit frantic. The haircut hadn't worked.

"Don't worry, Tatia," she blurted. "We could still try tears. I can chop some onions and cry lots and lots. But first, let me make you more hair."

She waved her wand. Once, twice . . . TWENTY times. Uh-oh! Sparkly hair flowed from Tatia like a silvery river.

"No. NO. N—*NEIGH*!" cried Tatia. "No more, Mai!"

Tatia reared up and, with a toss of her head, galloped away, her hair trailing behind her like the tail of a comet.

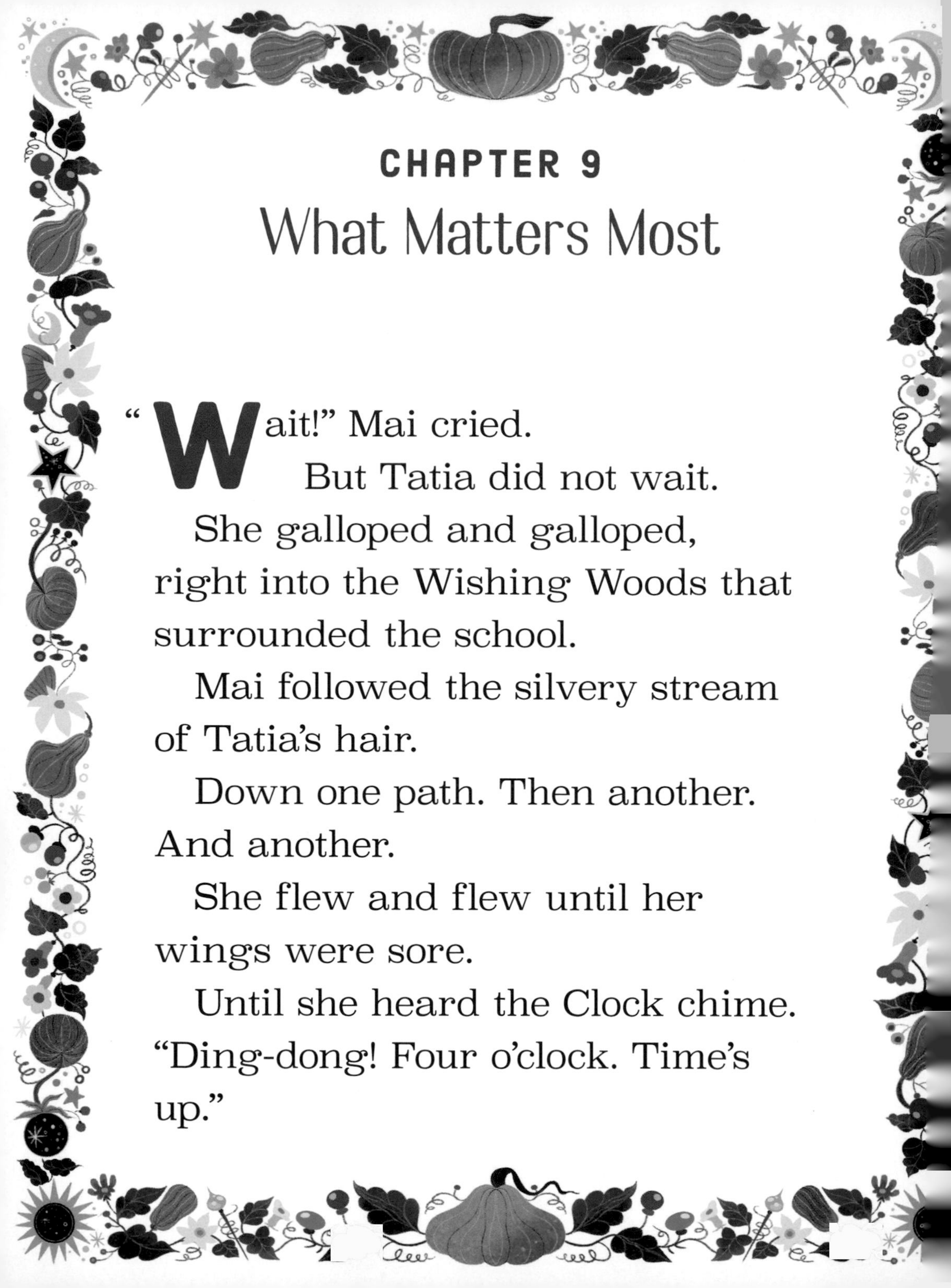

CHAPTER 9

What Matters Most

"Wait!" Mai cried.

But Tatia did not wait.

She galloped and galloped, right into the Wishing Woods that surrounded the school.

Mai followed the silvery stream of Tatia's hair.

Down one path. Then another. And another.

She flew and flew until her wings were sore.

Until she heard the Clock chime. "Ding-dong! Four o'clock. Time's up."

Until there were no more paths.
Where was Tatia?
Mai sat down in a slump.

After a while it grew dark. The ball had begun. She hadn't completed her magical assignment—again. There was no chance for a star. She had done the most she had ever done, and it *still* wasn't enough.

For once, Mai didn't feel bright.

But then, in the distance, she saw something else that was.

Tatia!

Tatia sat in a clearing, surrounded by silvery hair. Yet, she looked very small and very sad.

Mai landed softly beside her. When she saw Mai, she whinnied, "Go away."

"But," began Mai. "I want to . . ."

"Do *more*?" huffed Tatia.

"No," said Mai. "Say sorry. This is all my fault. I didn't listen. No more. Never ever again. I am changing my motto."

Tatia was quiet for a long moment. Then she slowly said, "But . . . no one is more sparkly than you. Or has more ideas. *More* is a perfect motto for you."

"Really?" said Mai.

"*Really*," said Tatia. "But more doesn't always mean better. And . . . neither does being first. I don't *always* need to be first. It's just . . . at home, I never get to be. I really wanted to earn a star. My sister has so many. And I haven't even completed *one* assignment."

Mai nodded. Above them, the stars twinkled. Real stars, full of real wishes. The kind that *really* mattered.

"I wanted a star, too. So everyone could see that I am a good fairy godmother," said Mai. "But . . . I would rather *be* a good fairy godmother."

"Me too," said Tatia. "Except I am not a fairy godmother anymore, not even in training. I'm a unicorn . . . with REALLY long hair. . . ."

Mai scooted closer to Tatia. Surely the teachers could fix her. But . . . what if they *couldn't*? What if she was a unicorn . . . forever?

"Oh, Tatia." Mai forgot all about completing more assignments, making more coaches, or getting more stars. She only had one wish: that she could help her friend.

A single tear filled Mai's eye.

The tear fell, bright as a star, right onto Tatia.

CHAPTER 10
The Star

Poof!

A cloud of sparkles and silvery hair filled the air, blinding Mai.

When it cleared, all that remained was a fairy.

Tatia!

"Oh my godmother!" exclaimed Tatia.

"My tear!" said Mai, amazed. "But it was only *one* tear."

"One was all I needed," said Tatia.

“I did *really* mean it,” said Mai.

Mai had undone a transformation for the first time. Maybe less was more, sometimes. Maybe the most magical transformations didn’t come from a wand, no matter how twinkly. They came from the heart.

The two fairy-godmothers-in-training arrived at the Story Shed, just as the princesses and princes were leaving—on foot!

"Tra-la-la." The princes and princesses were singing and laughing.

"Well, at least they aren't upset. But we *definitely* failed," said Mai.

"Failed? Why ever would you think that, my dear?" came a charming voice.

It was the Fairy Godmother! And Ms. Merryfeather was there, too.

"Well, because—" started Mai, with a gulp. She was about to say *because we didn't do anything*.

But the Fairy Godmother spoke first. "Because, of course, you earned your star."

"They did?" Ms. Merryfeather asked, surprised.

"We did?" Tatia asked, just as surprised.

"Now, where DID I put that slippery thing?" the Fairy Godmother muttered. "Oh! I forgot. I put it away!" She waved her wand, and a star appeared. Just one, to share. Still, it was perfect.

"B-but—" stammered Mai.

"Tell me," said the Fairy Godmother. "Did you learn about transformations?"

"A lot," said Tatia.

Mai nodded. "*More* than a lot."

"You see?" The Fairy Godmother gave them a knowing wink. "But the night's not done. It's time for you to have some fun."

"I thought the ball was over?" said Tatia.

"Not quite. Your friends are waiting for you."

In fact, just as the Fairy Godmother said this, the door to the Story Shed opened, and out peeked Rory, Cyrus, Ophelia, and the rest of the class.

"There you are!" they exclaimed. They were all waving their wands excitedly.

"Have we got a story to tell you!" said Rory. "Princes and princesses can cause so many problems. Come on!"

"You first," said Tatia, smiling at Mai.

Mai smiled back.

"In you go, dears," said the Fairy Godmother. "I'm sure they want to hear all about your adventure, too. And I think there are still cupcakes left that could use some more Bibbidi Bobbidi Boo."

"*Really?*" asked Mai.

"Really," said the Fairy Godmother.

"Like sprinkles!" said Mai. "And icing. And cherries . . ."

When it came to cupcakes, Mai's motto was *definitely* more.

Don't miss Bibbidi Bobbidi Academy Book 3:

Ophelia and the Fairy Field Trip

Coming Soon!